BEGINNING COUNTRY HARP

WITH CHARLIE McCOY

Wise Publications
London/New York/Paris/Sydney/Copenhagen/Madrid

Exclusive Distributors:
Music Sales Limited
8/9 Frith Street,
London W1V 5TZ, England.

Music Sales Pty Limited
120 Rothschild Avenue,
Rosebery, NSW 2018, Australia.

Music Sales Corporation
257 Park Avenue South,
New York, NY10010,
United States of America.

Order No. AM91710
ISBN 0-7119-3832-6
This book © Copyright 1994 by Wise Publications

All music examples © Copyright 1994
Dorsey Brothers Music Limited,
8/9 Frith Street,
London W1V 5TZ
All Rights Reserved.
International Copyright Secured.

Book design by 4i Limited, London
Compiled by Charlie McCoy
Edited by Pat Conway

Music processed by Seton Music Graphics
Photographs courtesy M. Hohner Co.

The publisher wishes to thank Martin Häffner and Christopher Wagner for use of their story
'The Harmonica in Country and Folk Music' from the book 'Made In Germany - Played In The USA'
published by the Hohner Harmonica Museum, Trossingen.

Music Sales' complete catalogue describes thousands of titles and is available in full colour sections by
subject, direct from Music Sales Limited. Please state your areas of interest and send a cheque/postal order
for £1.50 for postage to: Music Sales Limited, Newmarket Road, Bury St. Edmunds, Suffolk IP33 3YB.

Your Guarantee of Quality
As publishers, we strive to produce every book to the highest commercial standards.
The music has been freshly engraved and this book has been carefully designed to
minimise awkward page turns and to make playing from it a real pleasure.
Throughout, the printing and binding have been planned to ensure a sturdy,
attractive publication which should give years of enjoyment.
If your copy fails to meet our high standards, please inform us and we will
gladly replace it.

Printed in the United Kingdom

CONTENTS

SPECIAL THANKS

To my wife Pat, who got me started on this book and who kept me going
until it was finished. She also put it into plain English for me.

To my Mother, for all the love and the 50 cents she put up for my first harp.

To my Dad, who still loved me after I broke his heart by dropping out of college.
He was very proud of all my musical accomplishments.

To my two wonderful kids Ginger, and Charlie,
whose laughter brought real music to my life.

To Pat Conway, for helping put this book in order.

The main musical influences in my young life; Margaret DeSola,
my chorus teacher for 5 years. Elon Kealoha, my first guitar teacher,
Shirley Vinyard, my first music theory teacher; Madame Renée Longée,
who made music theory fun and made it make sense, and to
Happy Harold who introduced me to "country".

To my bands, The Charlie McCoy Band, The United, The Tomboola Band,
and The Tennessee 5.

To the Nashville people who believed in me; Mel Tillis, Jim Denny, Archie Bleyer,
Fred Foster, Sam Lovullo, Ray Pennington and Ted Fuller.

To Wayne Moss, for getting it on tape, and to Tex Davis, for telling the world.

To my great friend in Japan, Kenji Nagatomi.

To my early session influences; Chet Atkins, for hiring an unknown kid,
to Harold Bradley, for making me feel like I belonged, to Grady Martin,
the greatest session leader I have ever worked for, and to "Pig" Robbins,
the greatest session man I have ever known.

MY HISTORY WITH THE HARP

When I was 8 years old, growing up in Southern West Virginia, I saw an ad in a comic book "You too can play harmonica in 7 days". So I conned my Mother out of 50 cents, and with the 'right box top', I sent off for my first harmonica.

When the package arrived and my Mother heard the noisy wheezing, she banished me to the porch. This was bad news for all the four legged critters in the neighbourhood, both canine and feline.

After failing to produce anything musical for the first few days I resorted to the instructions. (This was a novel idea for an 8 year old.) There were 4 songs with instructions to "blow" and "draw" with the numbers of the holes.

Playing one note at a time was a problem at first, but drinking "pop" through a straw had trained me for this. After I figured out that the numbers were there for a reason, I managed to crank out "Old Folks At Home". I soon had a repertoire of 4 songs. My Mother was both proud and puzzled. How could this kid who couldn't remember to tie his shoes, remember 4 songs?

That Christmas, I got a guitar. I wanted to be another Gene Autry or Roy Rogers, who were popular cowboy singers at the time, so the harp was relegated to the sock drawer.

With the help of an uncle, I soon learned to play the chords to "Home On The Range". I wasn't ready for the stage yet though, because when my Mother "volunteered" me to sing and play for a school play, I "de-strung" my guitar with 6 easy snips of the wire cutters. The spanking didn't hurt half as bad as spending the rest of the summer without guitar strings.

My Mother and Dad had divorced, and after the 3rd grade, I spent the winters in Miami with my Dad, and the summers in West Virginia with my Mother. My dad was unpacking my suitcase and found my new harp. To my surprise, he picked it up and played a song. That briefly fired up my interest in the harp again, at least until football season began.

In 1955, Rock and Roll hit the radio like an epidemic, and all the kids with guitars wanted to be another Elvis. In Florida they were slow to get into R&B music on the radio. We were listening to Elvis, Pat Boone, Carl Perkins, and Guy Mitchell.

Contd p. 32

HOW TO HOLD
THE HARMONICA

You will notice that your harmonica has the numbers 1 - 10 on one side. Hold the instrument in your left hand with the number one, which is the lowest note, to the left. Place your right hand in the position shown below.

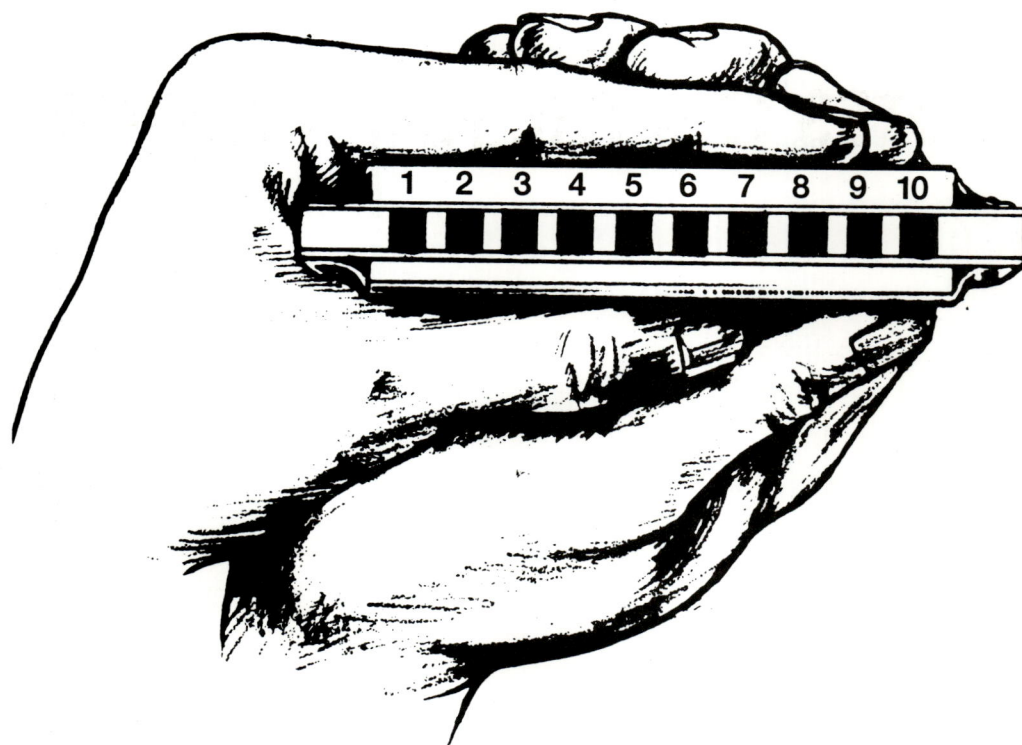

LET'S LOOK AT THE HARP

People ask "what key do you play in?" Well, there are twelve of them. However, for this book I am going to deal only with the "C" harp.
As you will need to use only one harp throughout this Tutor I strongly recommend you buy one of the Hohner models. They are the ones I use.
There are twenty notes available on any ten hole harp.
Ten holes with blow and draw on each hole.

To indicate breath direction, whether we blow or draw in our breath, I am going to use violin bow or guitar pick markings.

SIGNS AND SYMBOLS
USED IN THIS BOOK

⊓   Indicates a blow note (exhale).

V   Indicates a draw note (inhale).

③   A half circle underneath the music indicates a semitone (half step) bend.

③   A full circle underneath the music indicates a full tone (full step) bend.

NOTES ON THE HARMONICA

1	2	3	4	5	6	7	8	9	10
C D	E G	G B	C D	E F	G A	B C	D E	F G	A C

⊓ V   ⊓ V   ⊓ V   ⊓ V   ⊓ V   ⊓ V   V ⊓   ⊓ V   ⊓ V   V ⊓

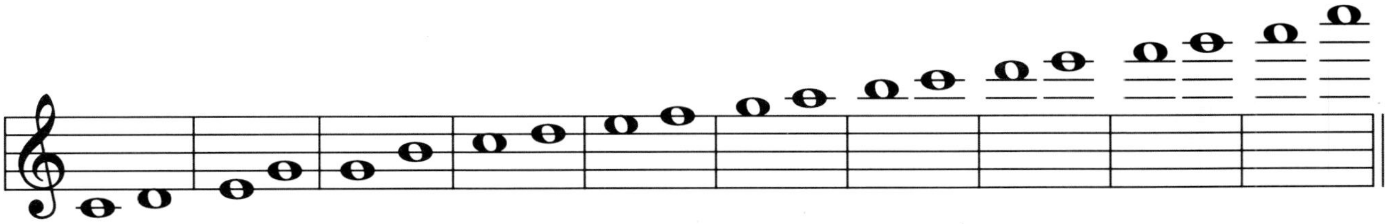

PLAY A SCALE

The first thing we learn to play on the harmonica is the C scale.
Try to play each note clearly without interference from neighbouring notes.
This may be tedious at first, but with a little practice you will soon
be able to play each individual note.

THE 'C' SCALE

Ex. 1

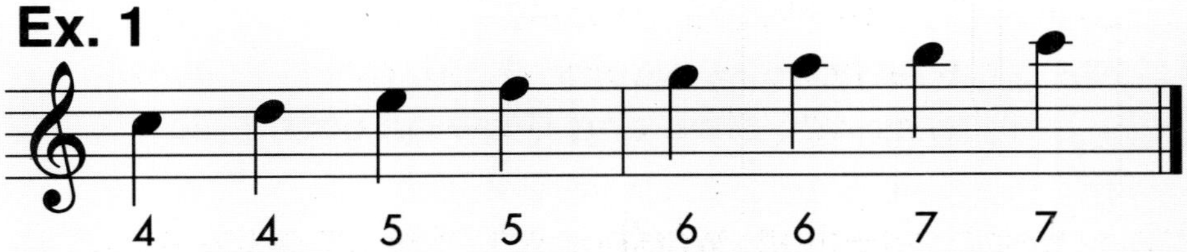

4   4   5   5   6   6   7   7

⊓ V   ⊓ V   ⊓ V   V ⊓

STRAIGHT PLAYING

This type of playing is called "Straight Playing" because the tunes are played in the natural key of the harmonica.
For example, with the C harmonica we will play in the key of C.

Although this is a country book which features mainly note bending, we have included three straight tunes. This is just to allow you to become familiar with the notes on the harmonica. All of the exercises and solos in this book will be played on the C harmonica.

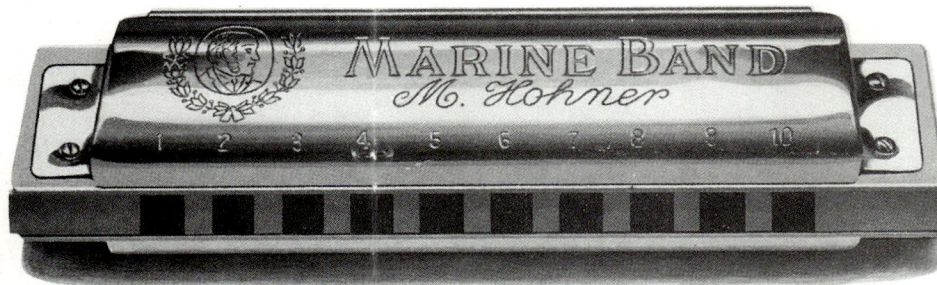

The ten-hole harmonica was allegedly discovered by a worker named Richter from Bohemia in 1857.
The following article in the Zeitschrift (No. 24 1882) reported that the company was already based in Haid(a), Bohemia in 1828 and was relocated to Regensburg, Bayern 1887.

The origins of the single-tone harmonica, which was fundamental to Blues and was so successful in America, are to be found in Bohemia. The Richter harmonica, an historical instrument in itself, is the original model for the 'Marine Band' as manufactured by Hohner since 1896. The name derives from the once most popular orchestra of the US Marine Corps. This is one of the best sellers in America. In its heyday in the late 1920s over a million 'Marine Bands' were sold each year in the US.

OLD FOLKS AT HOME

This is the first song I ever learned to play. Remember to find the hole number, and then see if it is a "blow"(⊓) note or a "draw" (V) note.

Charlie McCoy

AMERICA

Now let's look at another song that is very easy to play in the straight
harp style. This is called "America". However, in England
it is known as "God Save the Queen". Make sure you can play
each note clearly. If you can't do this well, slow it down.
Remember it is more important to play slowly and
accurately than to play a fast mess of notes.

VIBRATO

Vibrato is a technique that will make songs sound like music instead of whistling teapots. This is very effective and perhaps the easiest of all techniques to perform.

To do this, move your free hand as you play, right hand if you hold the harp with your left, and left hand if you hold the harp with your right.

At first you'll probably wonder, "how fast" should the vibrato be. As you play, you will find what is comfortable and what sounds the best to you.

Harmonica label, about 1930.

THE HARMONICA IN COUNTRY MUSIC

What Blues were to the blacks in the South, Hillbilly music was to the whites. In the 19th century, mostly fiddles rang out in the hills from Kentucky to Tennessee. Old dance melodies, brought by English and Scottish settlers, were put to music on the fiddle.

At the turn of the century the banjo and the harmonica found their way to the Appalachian mountains where they quickly became popular, although the fiddle remained the main instrument. The first record release with Hillbilly music came from Charlie Oaks and George Reneu in the mid-1920s. (Cf.C.Wolfe, 1977, p.30-1). They were two blind street singers who accompanied their songs with a guitar and a harmonica. The harp was mounted on a frame and worn around the neck.

Contd p. 15

SHENANDOAH

Now that you are familiar with Vibrato let's play my very favourite song, the beautiful American folk song "Shenandoah".
Leave out the Vibrato if you have difficulty playing the tune and the Vibrato at the same time. When you become comfortable with the tune and can play it with ease, then add the Vibrato. This will greatly enhance the melody.

CROSS PLAYING

Cross Playing means playing in a key other than the natural key of the harmonica. We can, by bending notes, play in many keys. However, throughout the rest of this book we will be playing 'crossed' mostly in the key of G.

The Cross Playing method is widely used in Rock, Country, Folk, and especially the Blues, as it allows for more tone control and individual expression.

One of the main reasons why the Cross Playing sound is so exciting is because of the constant use of 'note bending', which is what this book is all about.

CROSS HARP POSITIONS

Although it is possible to play in many keys on the harmonica as shown on this chart, you will find that the second position is the one most often used. We have used the 'C' harmonica for this book.

HARP KEY	STRAIGHT HARP 1st Position	CROSS HARP POSITIONS				
		2nd Position	3rd Position	4th Position	5th Position	6th Position
A	A	E	B	C# - Db	F# - Gb	D
Bb	Bb	F	C	D	G	Eb
B	B	F# - Gb	C# - Db	Eb	G# - Ab	E
C	C	G	D	E	A	F
Db	Db - C#	Ab - G#	Eb	F	Bb	F# - Gb
D	D	A	E	F# - Gb	B	G
Eb	Eb	Bb	F	G	C	Ab - G#
E	E	B	F# - Gb	G# - Ab	C# - Db	A
F	F	C	G	A	D	Bb
F#	F#	C# - Db	Ab - G#	Bb	Eb	B
G	G	D	A	B	E	C
Ab	Ab	Eb	Bb	C	F	C# - Db

The 4th, 5th and 6th positions are seldom used.

NOTE BENDING

'Note bending' is an essential part of playing the country harp.
You may find this technique slightly difficult at first.
However, with a little practice it will get easier.

'Note bending' may require the use of the tongue in much the same way as whistling. While drawing in your breath, try whistling a scale from the top note down to the bottom note. You will feel your tongue moving backwards as you descend the scale.

Try whistling the scale a few times and you will see what I mean.

Harmonica label, about 1910.

With the rise of radio as a mass medium in the 20s, a radio show which originated in Nashville, Tennessee, became extremely popular because it played live performances by musicians. The Grand Ole Opry became the nucleus and platform of American Country music. One of its first stars was Dr. Humphrey Bate, whose first group originated around the turn of the century. (Cf. C. Wolfe, 1977 -59-60). Bate was not the only harp musician in Tennessee, on the contrary, the region was an Eldorado for harmonica players and groups. The most famous were Charley Melton, who was named The French Harp King, and The Crook Brothers who had two harmonicas in the band. (Cf. C. Wolfe, 1977, p.60). A musician just as popular was Deford Bailey. His speciality was in replicating the sounds of fox chases and trains with his instrument like his Blues colleague Sonny Terry. He could make the harmonica bark like a dog, gallop like horses, and toot and puff like a steam train. (Cf. C. Wolfe, 1977, P.63). *Contd p. 29*

D TO D♭ BEND

Now let's start on hole number 4, and practice bending the note.
On our "C" harp, the note is "D" and it will bend down
to "D♭". This is a great note for playing the blues.
It can sound emotional and imitate crying.
This is also a good note to imitate a train, the wind, or a baby.

Remember to get a good "pucker" on the number 4 hole. While you're holding
the pitch, pull your tongue back and down from the opening of your mouth while
applying more pressure from your jaws.

Exercise Five is a basic bending exercise on hole number 4.
After you have bent the note, remember to
return it to its original pitch.

Ex. 5

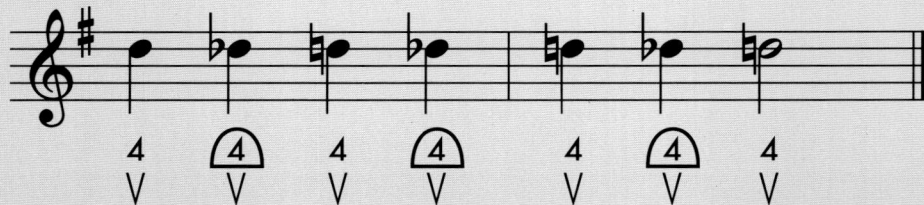

We are now going to add another note, so there will be a
little variety to the 4th hole bend.

Ex. 6

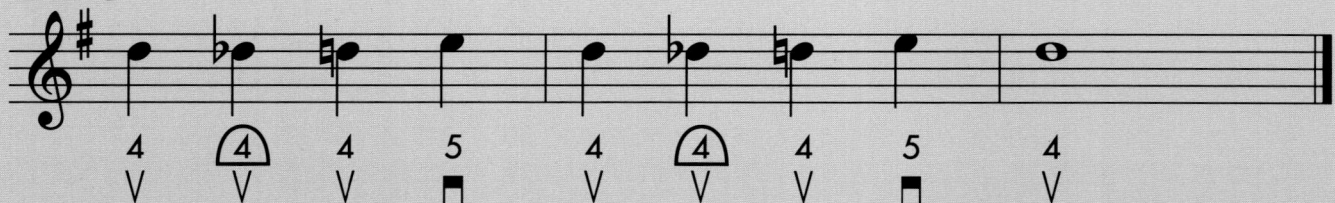

It is very important that you can play these exercises with ease before
moving on. A lot of people find that although it's quite easy to bend a
note on its own, it's another matter to play it within a solo.

FLAT THE FIVE

This is a bouncy little number featuring the D to D♭ bend.
If you have been successful with the last two exercises, then
you should have no great difficulty with this simple tune.

B TO B♭ BEND

If we draw in our breath on the third hole we will get the
note of B which we are going to bend down to B♭.
The principle is the same as before.

Here is the basic third hole bend exercise.

Ex. 8

3   ③   3   ③   3   ③   3

We will now add some extra notes for the next exercise.

Ex. 9

3   ③   3   4   3   ③   3   4   4   4   3   ③   3
V   V   V   ⊓   V   V   V   ⊓   V   V   V   V   V

Hand carved Harmonica, 1885.

Hand engraved Harmonica, 1860.

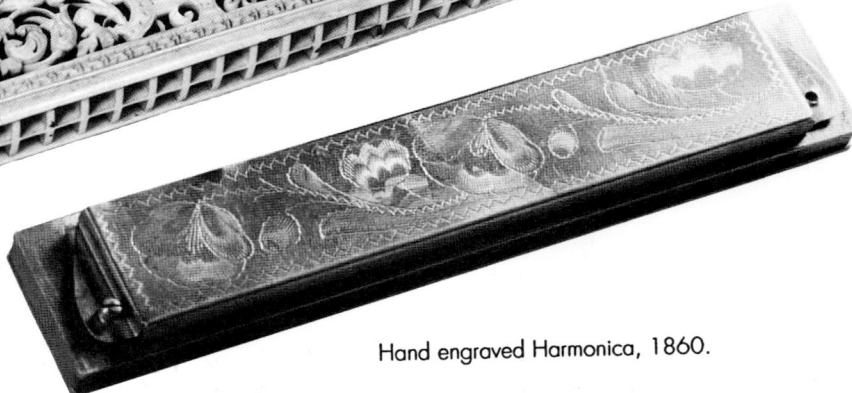

CHICKEN SCRATCH

Here is another tune using the B to Bb bend.
You may find this slightly more difficult than the last tune
as it contains more blow and draw notes in quick succession.
It should be played up tempo but you may slow it down if you wish.
Remember, it's more important to play with accuracy
than speed... speed will come with practice.

G to F♯ BEND

Drawing in your breath on the second hole, play the note of G. Then, using the note bending technique bend it down a half tone to F♯.

Here are some exercises for you to practice.

Ex. 11

We will now add some extra notes.

Ex. 12

RELATIVE MINOR CHART

HARP KEY	CROSS HARP KEY (2nd position)	RELATIVE MINOR KEY
A	E	C♯m
B♭	F	Dm
B	F♯ or G♭	D♯m or E♭m
C	G	Em
C♯ or D♭	G♯ or A♭	Fm
D	A	F♯m or G♭m
D♯ or E♭	A♯ or B♭	Gm
E	B	G♯m or A♭m
F	C	Am
F♯ or G♭	C♯ or D♭	A♯m or B♭m
G	D	Bm
G♯ or A♭	E♭	Cm

A MINOR PROBLEM

Here is a song in a minor key which features the G to F# bend.
You can see now by using bends, how a whole range of keys is available
to us. If you have been successful with the last two solos, you
should have no problem at all with this one.

BENT POLKA

This lively tune features the three half tone bends we
have just learned. D to D♭, B to B♭ and G to F♯.

Up to now the solos have featured only one bend, and if you can play them quite
easily then you should be ready for this one.
Most people find that playing more than one bend in the same solo can be
slightly difficult at first, so don't worry if you make a few mistakes initially.

BUILDING SPEED

Here are some runs to help build your speed. It is especially helpful if
you want to play "Bluegrass" music in the future.
You may be pleased to find that these runs have no bends.
Now I know you'll want to sound as fast as I am or should I say faster....!
Well let me tell you my speed and accuracy came with many
years of playing, it didn't happen overnight.

Ex. 15

2 3 4 5 6 5 4 3   2 3 4 5 6 5 4 3   2 3 4 5 6 5 4 3   2
V V V ⊓ ⊓ ⊓ V V   V V V ⊓ ⊓ ⊓ V V   V V V ⊓ ⊓ ⊓ V V   V

Ex. 16

3 4 5 6 6 6 5 4   3 4 5 6 6 6 5 4   3 4 5 6 6 6 5 4   3
V V V ⊓ V ⊓ V V   V V V ⊓ V ⊓ V V   V V V ⊓ V ⊓ V V   V

Ex. 17

4 5 6 6 7 6 6 5   4 5 6 6 7 6 6 5   4 5 6 6 7 6 6 5   4
V ⊓ ⊓ V V V ⊓ ⊓   V ⊓ ⊓ V V V ⊓ ⊓   V ⊓ ⊓ V V V ⊓ ⊓   V

Ex. 18

1 2 2 3 4 5 5 6 6 6 5 5 4 4 3 2   1 2 2 3 4 5 5 6 6 6 5 5 4 4 3 2   2
V ⊓ V V V V ⊓ V ⊓ V ⊓ V ⊓ V ⊓ V V   V ⊓ V V V V ⊓ V ⊓ V ⊓ V ⊓ V ⊓ V V   V

Ex. 19

4 5 6 6 7 8 7 6 6 7 6 5 4 5 4   4 5 6 6 7 8 7 6 6 7 6 7 6
V ⊓ ⊓ V V V V V ⊓ ⊓ V ⊓ V ⊓ V   V ⊓ ⊓ V V V V V ⊓ ⊓ V ⊓ V ⊓

23

Charlie McCoy on stage with the Nashville Pops Orchestra

SPEED RUNS WITH BENDS

Here are some more runs to help you build speed. These include some of the half tone bends which we have learned so far.

Ex. 20

1 2 2 3 4 5 6 5   4 (4) 4 4 3   1 2 2 3 4 5 6 5   4 (4) 4 4 3 2
V ∏ V V V ∏ ∏ ∏   V V ∏ V V   V ∏ V V V ∏ ∏ ∏   V V ∏ V V V

Ex. 21

3 (3) 3 4 4 (4) 4 5   5 5 4 4 3   3 (3) 3 4 4 (4) 4 5   4 (4) 4 3 2
V V V ∏ V V V V   V ∏ V ∏ V   V V V ∏ V V V V   V ∏ V ∏ V V

Ex. 22

6 5 4 5 4 (4) 4 4   3 (3) 3 4 3   6 5 4 5 4 (4) 4 3   4 3 2 (2) 2
∏ ∏ V V ∏ V   V V   V V V V V   ∏ ∏ V V ∏ V V   V V V V V

Ex. 23

4 5 6 6 7 6 6 5   4 (4) 4 4 3   7 6 6 5 4 (4) 4 4   3 (3) 3 1 2
V ∏ ∏ V ∏ V V V   V V ∏ ∏ V   V ∏ V ∏ ∏ V V   V V V V V V

Ex. 24

1 2 2 3 4 5 5 6   6 7 7 6 7   7 6 6 5 5 4 (4) 4   3 1 2 (2) 2
V ∏ V V V ∏ V ∏   V V ∏ V V   V ∏ V ∏ V ∏ V ∏   V V V V V

FULL TONE BENDS

Now let's stretch the limits of the harp even more by bending full steps. This is extremely important in country music as you will be playing mainly melodies. It is imperative that you can get the note of A on the third hole with ease.

B TO A BEND

So far we have been dealing with half tone bends, now we will learn how to perform full tone bends.

A word of caution at this stage. It's easy to misjudge the intonation. This may be done by bending a half tone instead of a full tone or by bending the note down three half tones instead of a full tone.

Drawing in your breath on the third hole of the harmonica, play the note B. Using the 'note bending' technique, bend this note down a half tone to B♭, then continue bending it down further until you reach the note A.

Now, perform the same bend again, only this time bend it down a full tone from B to A without stopping at the half tone.

You may find full tone bends slightly more difficult to perform than the half tone bend, as it may involve further backward movement of the tongue. Practice these exercises before moving on to the solo.

For this next exercise we will first bend a half tone then continue down to a full tone. This will let you hear the difference between a half tone bend and a full tone bend.

Ex. 25

27

In this next exercise you will have to bend a full tone B to A without stopping at the half tone bend. This is a little more difficult.

Ex. 26

Ex. 27

Here is another exercise featuring the B to A bend.

FULL BENDS

Now let's play a song incorporating the B to A bend. Although there are no other bends used in this piece, you may still find the full tone bend B to A difficult to do within a tune.

Ex. 28

SMOKIN' IN THE SMOKIES

This tune should be played rather quickly. It contains the B to A bend on the third hole and again there are no other bends used.

At the end of the 40s, when Hillbilly music was renamed Country & Western, it gained more importance in popular music. Musicians, such as Dynamite Hatcher from Roy Acuff's Crazy Tennesseans, Wayne Rainey and Lonnie Glosson from The Delmore Brothers, carried on the tradition of the harmonica. Later, younger harp players, such as Jimmy Riddle, Onie Wheeler and Charlie McCoy walked in their footsteps. The emergence of Rock'n'Roll and Rock music in the 50s and 60s did not leave Country music untouched. Johnny Cash (singer, guitarist, and harmonica player) worried less about style boundaries and combined acoustic guitar sounds with electric Rock'n'Roll. In the 70s, Southern bands such as The Ozark Mountain Dare Devils, The Nitty Gritty Dirt Band, or The Marshall Tucker Band, turned the volume up even louder, letting their E-guitar howl with a hard rock rhythm drum beat. Country Rock became known as a new style and the sound of the harmonica rang out, thus making the harmonica an integral part of country music.

G TO F BEND

Drawing in your breath on the second hole of the harmonica,
play the note of G. Bend this note down a half tone to F♯,
then continue bending until you reach the note of F.

Now perform the bend again, only this time bend the note straight
down from G to F without stopping at the half tone bend.

Ensure that your intonation is correct and that you can perform
this full tone bend before going on to the solo.

Here is the basic G to F bend exercise.

Ex. 30

We have now added some more notes for this next exercise.

Ex. 31

This exercise has still more notes for you to try.

Ex. 32

THE SEVENTH DAY

You may notice that as we progress the solos are getting tougher. This tune is no exception as it contains not only the G to F bend, but also the B to A bend.

31

BIG BAD BEND

Here is another solo using the G to F full tone bend on the second hole. If you can play the last tune then you should have no trouble with this.

Ex. 34

Contd from p.5

My next summer in West Virginia found all the kids talking, and breathing, music. We had discovered girls and were learning to dance. When I asked if they had heard "Long Tall Sally" by Pat Boone, they laughed. "Pat Boone, Florida must be the squarest place in the world".

"Haven't you ever heard of Little Richard?" They played some Little Richard, Fats Domino and Chuck Berry for me and I was converted.

When I returned to Florida with my new musical taste, I found that the radio was still segregated. Searching the radio I found an "R&B" station, and more importantly, I discovered Jimmy Reed.

My Dad worked for a furniture store on the edge of the black section of Miami, and one Saturday when he took me to work with him, I snuck out of the store and boldly ventured in search of a record store. My allowance went for "You Got Me Dizzy".

Contd p. 33

BOTH BENDS NOW

Here's a slow bluegrass style waltz, using both the second and third hole full tone bends. B to A and G to F.

When I got home, I discovered that my Dad's taste in music wasn't anything like mine, so I had to wait until he was gone to play my new record. One of my friend's Dad fixed up my clock radio with an earphone jack, so I could listen to the radio with earphones at night. I discovered a radio station called WLAC that played blues all night. I was introduced to Slim Harpo, Sonny Boy Williamson, and most importantly, Little Walter.

The station was in, of all places, Nashville, Tennessee. They were sponsored by mail-order record stores, so my allowance was sent to Nashville ordering records.

Some of my friends formed a band, and needed a guitar player. It was great to be in a band, until we had slight differences of opinion about what music we should play. They wanted Elvis, Pat Boone etc., and I wanted Little Richard and Jimmy Reed. JIMMY REED!! What I loved about Jimmy Reed was that haunting harp, and "I HAD A HARP".

Contd p. 39

33

DOUBLE TROUBLE

This tune is no more difficult than the previous solos even though it contains a
D to D♭ half tone bend, along with the B to A and G to F full tone bends.
If you can play this tune you should be real proud of yourself
having got this far. You should now be able to play almost
any tune, be it country, blues or whatever....

Ex. 35

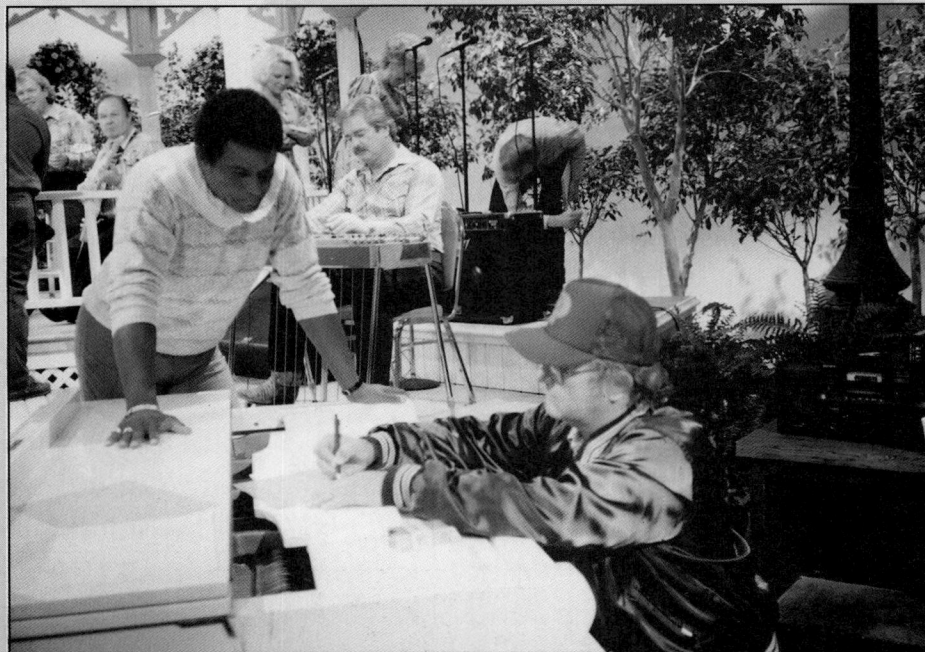

On the set of "Hee Haw" with country superstar Charley Pride

BLUEGRASS LICKS

Now I know at this stage you must be well able to play the full tone bends
B to A and G to F. If you had followed my advice about first playing slowly and
accurately and then building up speed, you are going to reap the benefit of it
now as these next "Bluegrass Licks" have to be played fast.

Ex. 37

Ex. 38

Ex. 39

Ex. 40

Ex. 41

OLDE JOE CLARKE

Here is a famous Bluegrass classic for you to try. It is usually played on the G banjo or fiddle and if you can play it on the harp then you can really impress your friends.

"Charles Ray" with Ray Charles

HAND ROLLS

This is a great technique for you to learn and very popular
in country music. Some people refer to these "hand rolls" as "trills".
The idea is to take two adjacent notes and move the harp very
quickly so the two notes sound alternately.

You need to have a pucker position and let your lips be a bit loose,
so that when you move the harp they are flexible.

In Exercise 43 we will start with holes two and three. Start with hole two in your
mouth in a pucker position. Move the harp very very slightly and rapidly from
side to side, it should be more like a quivering.

Again it is very important that no other notes except the two
which are involved should be heard.

Ex. 43

Now move up to holes 4 and 5.

Ex. 44

Now try holes 5 and 6.

Ex. 45

Finally, beginning on holes 3 and 4, we will roll 3 and 4,
then blow 4 and 5 both at the same time and then roll 4 and 5,
blow 5 and 6 at the same time and then roll 5 and 6,
blow 5 and 6 and finally roll 4 and 5.
Phew! I hope you got all that.

Ex. 46

Here is another exercise comprised of single notes,
rolls and double note playing.

Ex. 47

There were no instruction books or videos available then like that of Don Baker's complete harmonica techniques which I highly recommend you get. I just sat for hours trying to figure out what he was doing. Somehow, I figured out Jimmy Reed, so it was onto Slim, Sonny Boy, and Little Walter.

One of my friends talked me into going to a dance at the National Guard Armory. He didn't tell me that the music was country. (To a 17 year old in the 50s, country was "Squaresville".)

When we arrived at the door, I heard the music and was starting to turn back. He said, "let's just go listen a minute". When we entered, the whole crowd was in a big circle doing a square dance. I, the self-proclaimed expert on all that was cool, was amused at this act of "hill-billy mania".

In the meantime, my friend was at the stage asking the band to get me up to play and sing. I heard an introduction, "Friends, we've got a great guitar player and singer here tonight, so let's give him a big hand and get him up, Charlie McCoy". I wanted to kill my friend.

Contd p. 45

THE BLUES GIVES ME A THRILL

Here's a great little solo which makes use of the hand roll.
Practice this technique in some of the previous solos or in new tunes
which I'm sure you're trying at this stage.

DIRECT BENDING

This is a must and will elevate your playing to a new level and is
a very important technique for playing country music.
Direct Bending is playing a note already bent. For example,
playing D to D♭ where we go directly to D♭ then release
it upwards to D. Now the half tone ones are difficult enough
and you will certainly find the full tone ones a real challenge.
For example, on the third hole, bending the note of A up to B.

This is much more difficult than playing a note and then bending
it down which is with the tongue and jaw already in the "bent" mode,
then releasing the note upwards.

There is also a question of pitch. A lot of this technique is in the mind.
You have to imagine what the note sounds like in the bent position
and how it feels to bend it by the proper amount.

This is not easy so it will take persistence and patience.

Other 'Instrumentalist of the Year' nominees escort 'Pig' to the microphone
...Roy Clark, Chet Atkins, Johnnie Gimble and Charlie McCoy. Bill Anderson stands at the rear.

Ex. 49 features half tone direct bends D♭ up to D,
B♭ up to B and F♯ up to G.

Ex. 49

This one also features the same half tone bends.

Ex. 50

For Ex. 51 we will also add the B to A bend which is quite difficult.

Ex. 51

This next exercise contains only full tone bends A up to B and B down to A,
also the A down to G and G up to A.

Ex. 52

A COUNTRY LOVE SONG

Here is a slow country song which you may find very
difficult to play as it contains direct bends.

BIG WIND FROM LAYTOWN

This solo combines everything we've learned.
Good luck and keep on harping!

The applause was heavy so I just HAD to do it. But what would I play?
I borrowed a guitar and sheepishly asked the leader, "Do you know Johnny B. Goode?"
To my surprise he said "What key?" I said "A", and he said "Let'er rip".

The band was great. They were very helpful and not like the young jealous rock and rollers that I usually encountered. I must have done well because there were two encores. The audience was much more appreciative than the teenagers that I usually played for. Within the course of 3 songs, my musical outlook had been adjusted.

A year later, I went to work for Happy Harold and the "Old South Jamboree", playing rock and roll songs 15 minutes each set. Mel Tillis came in one night after a country show at the Dade Country Auditorium. When I came down from the stage he said, "So if you will come to Nashville, I can get you on Decca (the record label) tomorrow".

I asked Happy if Mel was for real, and he said that Mel was an important songwriter in Nashville, and I wouldn't take what he said too lightly.

Right after graduation from high school, Happy Harold took me to Nashville to see Mel. Mel was out of town, but he had told his manager, Jim Denny, about me. Denny took me to audition for Chet Atkins, Don Law, Jim Vienneau, and Owen Bradley. I set up an amp and played and sang "Johnny B. Goode". Owen Bradley told Denny "Well I think he's pretty good, but I don't know what to do with him". (Rock & Roll was not big in Nashville in 1959.)

Owen invited me to see a recording session. I watched a 13 year old girl named Brenda Lee record "Sweet Nuthins'". These musicians were the best I'd ever seen, and the ease with which they worked was amazing. I also met The Jordanaires (the same ones who sang with Elvis). I got a look at their music - nothing but numbers - the same stuff I had studied in high school theory.

Feeling like a whipped dog, I returned to Miami. "To heck with it, I'm going to be a music teacher". I had an experimental high school class in music theory, and I loved it, so I entered the University of Miami which has a great music school.

My fondest memory at University of Miami was a solfeggio teacher named Madame Renée Longée. (Solfeggio is ear training and sight singing.) She flunked Leonard Bernstein years earlier at Eastman School of Music, to wake him up, because she knew he was a genius and was goofing off. She got his attention, and the world of music was much better for it.

As my freshman year dragged on, the non-music subjects began to monopolize my time, taking away from studying music. The more time passed, the more I thought about that session in Nashville. One day, on the way to school, I pulled my car over and asked myself; "Where am I going, I don't want to teach, I want to play."

When I told my Dad, he was heartbroken. Sending his son to college was his dream, and the University of Miami was a heavy load for a blue-collar worker. He told me that I would starve, and run back to Miami soon. I think he just wanted me to be sure.

In April of '60, I got a call from Kent Westbury, a guy from the Old South who had gone to Nashville. He told me he was putting a band together for Johnny Ferguson, a guy with a hit song called "Angela Jones". We drove all night from Miami to Nashville, (without freeways) and arrived at the first rehearsal.

You can imagine my dismay when Johnny told Kent, "I didn't hear from you, so I already hired a guitar player." Feeling sorry for me Johnny asked, "what else do you play?" I said "I play harmonica". He said he didn't think he could use a harmonica but asked if I played drums. Way in the back of my thick skull a voice said, "say no, and your Nashville days will end before they begin." So I said "Yes, but I don't have any." He said we'll get you some.

Two weeks later, the gig was done, Johnny's second record was a bomb, and I was out of work, with a set of drums. Wayne Gray, another Old South grad, called and said he was putting together a band for Stonewall Jackson, and could I play drums. What else could I say? Yes of course.

One day, out on the road, Jim Denny called and said that Archie Bleyer, of Cadence Records had heard one of my demos, and wanted to talk to me about recording. Denny had me quit the road so I could be around when Archie needed me, and I started to work demo sessions on harp to pay Denny for keeping me in town. I recorded "Cherry Berry Wine" and it got to Number 99 in *Billboard* for 1 week. More important, I was doing sessions and playing harmonica instead of drums.

One August morning, Denny said "Chet Atkins heard one of the demos you played on, and he is going to record that song on a new artist named Ann-Margret. He wants you to play on it." This August day would be the beginning of two careers, Ann Margret, and Charlie McCoy, the studio musician. Bob Moore, a studio bass player on the session, asked me if I could work that Friday with Roy Orbison. ROY ORBISON! I loved him. We recorded "Candy Man" and I was off and running as a studio musician.

The harmonica has been my friend and provider, has associated me with the biggest stars in music, and has taken me around the world.

The one lesson I have learned is , "Dogs and cats have no taste", even after I learned to play good music, they still hate it.

47

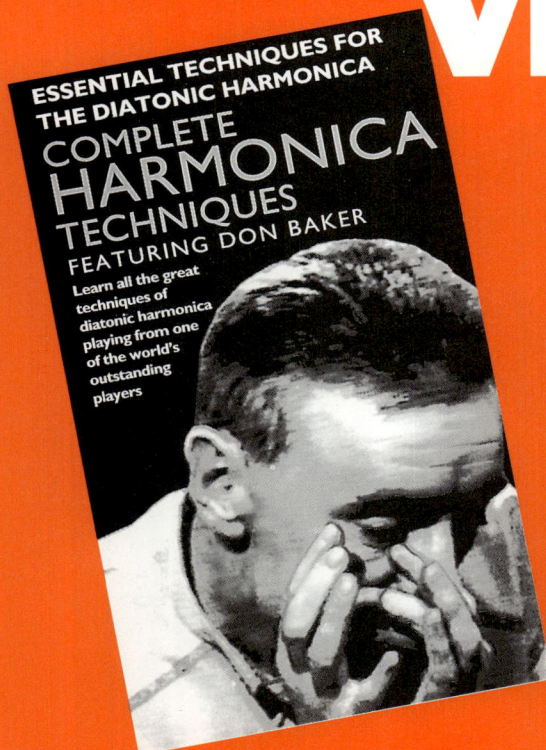